At the Carnival

adapted by Leslie Valdes
based on the script, "The Big Piñata"
illustrated by Robert Roper

SIMON AND SCHUSTER/NICKELODEON

Based on the TV series *Dora the Explorer* as seen on Nick Jr.

SIMON AND SCHUSTER
First published in Great Britain in 2007 by Simon & Schuster UK Ltd
Africa House, 64-78 Kingsway, London WC2B 6AH
A CBS Company

Originally published in the USA in 2003 by Simon Spotlight,
an imprint of Simon & Schuster Children's Division, New York.

A CIP catalogue record for this book is available from the British Library

ISBN-10: 1847380239
ISBN-13: 9781847380234
Printed in China

10 9 8 7 6 5 4 3 2 1

Visit our websites: www.simonsays.co.uk
www.nick.co.uk

Hi, I'm Dora. Do you like to play games? Me too! Boots and I are at a carnival. That's a festival where you play games and win prizes! Boots and I want to win the grand prize - the Big Piñata!

When a piñata breaks open, all kinds of prizes fall out - like toys and stickers and treats!

To win the Big Piñata we need to collect eight yellow tickets.
Will *you* help us win the Big Piñata? Great!

How do we get to the Big Piñata? Let's ask Map. Say "Map!"

"Hurry, hurry, hurry!" calls Map. "You have to go past the Ferris wheel, then go around the merry-go-round, and that's how you'll get to the Big Piñata."

Along the way we'll collect the eight yellow tickets by going on rides and playing games.

We made it to the Ferris wheel! Look – it's Señor Tucán! He says we can ride the Ferris wheel, but first we have to find an empty seat.

Will you help us find an empty seat on the Ferris wheel? What blue shape is next to it?

Yay! You found the empty seat next to the blue star! Señor Tucán says we have won four yellow tickets!

Now we can ride the Ferris wheel. Higher and higher and higher we go! Whee!

Next we'll go to the merry-go-round! Can you see it?

Here's Isa the iguana. Isa says that if we ride the merry-go-round and find the orange ring, we can win more yellow tickets.

Will *you* help us find the orange ring?
¡Excelente! You found it!

We just won four yellow tickets! Yay!
Let's see. We had four yellow tickets from before, and now we have won four more yellow tickets.

So how many tickets do we have altogether?
That's right – eight!

Now we can win the Big Piñata! Can you see it? Come on, we're almost there!

Uh-oh, that sounds like Swiper the fox! That sneaky fox will try to swipe our tickets!

Can you see Swiper? We have to say "Swiper, no swiping!"

Thanks for helping us stop Swiper. We made it to the Big Piñata!

"Step right up!" says the Fiesta Trio. "You need eight tickets to win."

We have eight tickets. *¡Fantástico!* We won the Big Piñata!

Look! All of our friends are here to help open the Big Piñata.

To open the Big Piñata we need to pull the green ribbon. Can you see the green ribbon? Reach out and grab it with both hands. Pull!

Hooray! We opened the Big Piñata! And look – there are toys and stickers and treats everywhere. Thanks for helping! *¡Adiós!*